93-02578

J398.8
RIN   16.95

Ring O' Roses.

Withdrawn

Ring O' Roses

Ring O' Roses

A Nursery Rhyme Picture Book

Illustrated by
L. Leslie Brooke

With an afterword by
Neil Philip

CLARION BOOKS

NEW YORK

Clarion Books
a Houghton Mifflin Company imprint
215 Park Avenue South, New York, NY 10003

An Albion Book

Designer: Andrew Shoolbred
Project Manager: Elizabeth Wilkes

This edition of RING O' ROSES has been newly originated from
Leslie Brooke's original watercolors and line drawings, which
are reproduced courtesy of the Brooke family. Seven missing
subjects have been reproduced from a first edition of 1922.

Library of Congress Cataloging-in-Publication Data

Mother Goose.
    Ring o' roses/L. Leslie Brooke.
      p. cm.
    Summary: An illustrated collection of twenty-one Mother Goose
nursery rhymes, including "Hickety Pickety My Black Hen," "The Three
Wise Men of Gotham," and "The Lion and the Unicorn."
    ISBN 0-395-61304-3
    1. Nursery rhymes. 2. Children's poetry.   [1. Nursery rhymes.]
    I. Brooke, L. Leslie (Leonard Leslie), 1862-1940. II. Title.
    PZ8.3.M85 1992
    J 398.8—dc20   91-27028
                                        CIP
                                        AC

00 10 9 8 7 6 5 4 3 2 1

Typesetting by York House Typographic, London
Color origination by Pressplan Reprographics Ltd, Watford
Printed and bound in Hong Kong by South China Printing Co.

Contents

Ring O' Roses   6

Humpty Dumpty   8

Cock-a-Doodle Doo   13

There was a Crooked Man   17

Oranges and Lemons   20

The Man in the Moon   25

There was a Man   28

Goosey, Goosey Gander   35

To Market, To Market   39

Baa, Baa Black Sheep   42

The Lion and the Unicorn   47

This Little Pig went to Market   51

Simple Simon   58

Hickety Pickety my Black Hen   63

Little Miss Muffet   66

The Three Wise Men of Gotham   70

There was a Little Man   74

Jack and Jill   77

Good King Arthur   81

Little Bo-Peep   85

Wee Willie Winkie   89

Afterword   92

Index of first lines   96

Ring O' Roses

Ring a ring o' roses,
    A pocket full of posies;
Hush! hush! hush!
    And we all tumble down.

Humpty Dumpty

Humpty Dumpty sat on a wall;

Humpty Dumpty had a great fall;

All the King's horses and all the King's men
Couldn't put Humpty Dumpty together again.

Cock-a-Doodle Doo

Cock-a-doodle doo!
My dame has lost her shoe;
My master's lost his fiddling-stick,
And don't know what to do.

Cock-a-doodle doo!
What is my dame to do?
Till master finds his fiddling-stick
She'll dance without her shoe.

Cock-a-doodle doo!
My dame has lost her shoe,
And master's found his fiddling-stick;
Sing doodle-doodle-doo!

Cock-a-doodle doo!
My dame will dance with you,
While master fiddles his fiddling-stick,
For dame and doodle-doo.

Cock-a-doodle doo!
Dame has lost her shoe;
Gone to bed and scratched her head.
And can't tell what to do.

There was a Crooked Man

There was a crooked man, and he went
    a crooked mile,
He found a crooked sixpence against a crooked
    stile:

He bought a crooked cat, which caught a
    crooked mouse,

And they lived together in a crooked
little house.

Oranges and Lemons

Gay go up, and gay go down
To ring the bells of London Town.

Bull's eyes and targets,
Say the bells of St. Marg'ret's.

Brickbats and tiles,
Say the bells of St. Giles'.

Pancakes and fritters,
Say the bells of St. Peter's.

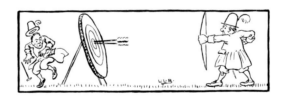

Two sticks and an apple,
Say the bells at Whitechapel.

Halfpence and farthings,
Say the bells of St. Martin's.

Oranges and Lemons,
Say the bells of St. Clement's.

Old Father Baldpate,
Say the slow bells at Aldgate.

Pokers and tongs,
Say the bells of St. John's.

Kettles and pans,
Say the bells of St. Ann's.

You owe me ten shillings,
Say the bells at St. Helen's.

When will you pay me?
Say the bells at Old Bailey.

When I grow rich,
Say the bells at Shoreditch.

Pray when will that be?
Say the bells of Stepney.

I am sure I don't know,
Says the great bell of Bow.

*Here comes a candle
to light you to bed,
And here comes a chopper
to chop off your head.*

The Man in the Moon

The Man in the Moon
    Came tumbling down,
And asked his way to Norwich;

They told him south,
And he burnt his mouth
With eating cold pease-porridge.

There was a Man

There was a man, and he had nought,
And robbers came to rob him;

He crept up to the chimney-pot,

AND THEN THEY THOUGHT THEY HAD HIM

BUT HE GOT DOWN ON T'OTHER SIDE

And then they could not find him;

He ran fourteen miles in fifteen days,
And never looked behind him.

Goosey, Goosey Gander

Goosey, Goosey Gander,
    Where shall I wander?

Upstairs, downstairs,
    And in my lady's chamber.

There I met an old man
That would not say his prayers:

I took him by the left leg,
And threw him downstairs.

To Market, To Market

To market, to market, to buy a fat Pig;
    Home again, home again, dancing a jig.

To market, to market, to buy a fat Hog;
    Home again, home again, jiggety-jog.

Baa, Baa Black Sheep

Baa, baa Black Sheep,
        Have you any wool?
Yes, marry, have I,
        Three bags full:

One for my master,
And one for my Dame,
And one for the little boy
That lives in the lane!

The Lion and the Unicorn

The Lion and the Unicorn
    Were fighting for the crown;
The Lion beat the unicorn
    All round about the town.

Some gave them white bread,
    And some gave them brown;
Some gave them plum-cake,
    And sent them out of town.

This Little Pig went to Market

This little pig went to market;

This little pig stayed at home;
This little pig had roast beef;

This little pig had none;

This little pig cried "Wee, wee, wee!

I   can't   find   my   way

home!"

Simple Simon

Simple Simon met a pieman,
　　Going to the fair;
Says Simple Simon to the pieman,
　　"Let me taste your ware."

Says the pieman to Simple Simon,
"Do you mean to pay?"
Says Simon, "Yes, of course I do!"
And then he ran away.

Simple Simon went a-fishing
For to catch a whale:
All the water he had got
Was in his mother's pail.

Hickety Pickety my Black Hen

Hickety pickety my black hen,
She lays eggs for gentlemen;

The sign reads: MRS. HICKETY PICKETY FRESH EGGS

Gentlemen come every day
To see what my black hen doth lay.

Little Miss Muffet

Little Miss Muffet
Sat on a tuffet

Eating of curds and whey;

There came a big Spider
And sat down beside her,

And frightened Miss Muffet away.

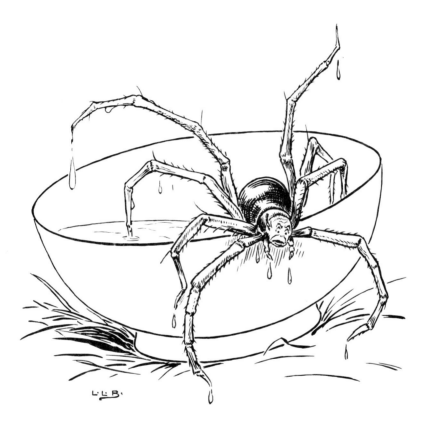

The Three Wise Men of Gotham

Three wise men of Gotham
Went to sea in a bowl:

If the bowl had been stronger,
    My song would have been longer.

There was a Little Man

There was a little man,
And he had a little gun,
And his bullets were made of lead, lead, lead;
He went to the brook
And saw a little duck,
And he shot it right through the head, head, head.

He carried it home
To his old wife Joan,
And bid her a fire for to make, make, make;
To roast the little duck
He had shot in the brook,
And he'd go and fetch her the drake, drake, drake.

Jack and Jill

Jack and Jill went up the hill
To fetch a pail of water;

Jack fell down and broke his crown,
And Jill came tumbling after.

Good King Arthur

When good king Arthur ruled this land,
    He was a goodly king;
He stole three pecks of barley-meal,
    To make a bag-pudding.

A bag-pudding the king did make,
　　And stuffed it well with plums:
And in it put great lumps of fat,
　　As big as my two thumbs.

The king and queen did eat thereof,
　　And noblemen beside;
And what they could not eat that night,
　　The queen next morning fried.

Little Bo-Peep

Little Bo-Peep has lost her sheep,
    And can't tell where to find them;
Leave them alone, and they'll come home,
    And bring their tails behind them.

Little Bo-Peep fell fast asleep,
    And dreamt she heard them bleating;
But when she awoke, she found it a joke,
    For they were still a-fleeting.

Then up she took her little crook,
    Determined for to find them;
She found them indeed, but it made her heart bleed,
    For they'd left all their tails behind 'em.

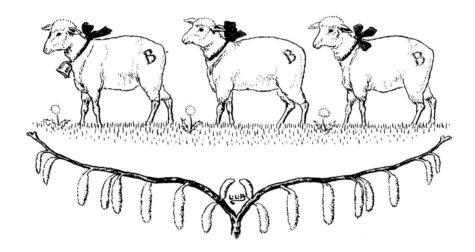

Wee Willie Winkie

Wee Willie Winkie runs through the town,
Upstairs and downstairs in his nightgown,
Rapping at the window, crying through the lock,

"Are the children in their beds, for now it's eight o'clock?"

Leslie Brooke is one of the most important children's illustrators of the twentieth century. The verve of his line and the robustness of his humor quickly established his reputation as, in the words of Maurice Sendak, "a spiritual descendant of Caldecott."

He was born Leonard Leslie Brooke in Birkenhead, Cheshire, England, on September 24, 1862, and studied art at Birkenhead Art School and subsequently at the St. John's Wood Art School and the Royal Academy Art Schools in London.

On completing his training, he began to undertake book illustrations for various publishers. In 1891 he took over from Walter Crane as the regular illustrator of books by Mrs. Molesworth, one of the leading children's writers of the day.

The book which made his name, and linked him for the rest of his career with the firm of Warne, who published all his important books, was *The Nursery Rhyme Book*, edited by Andrew Lang. This glorious collection of traditional rhymes contained over a hundred black-and-white drawings of unusual energy, wit, and lyricism. The book was a great success, partly no doubt because of Lang's prestigious name on the title page, though it was Leslie Brooke himself who had selected the rhymes.

Warne followed up *The Nursery Rhyme Book* with two selections of nonsense poems by Edward Lear, *The Pelican Chorus* and *The Jumblies*, which were the first and are possibly still the best attempt by another hand to illustrate Lear's zany and oddly wistful rhymes. For these books, which were later combined into one volume, Leslie Brooke was allowed to supplement his line drawings with color plates.

The mixture of color and black-and-white illustrations in the Lear books was repeated in even more lavish abundance in Leslie Brooke's *The Golden Goose Book* (1905) and *Ring O' Roses* (1922), which

Virginia Haviland, first Head of the Children's Book Section of the Library of Congress, has described as "irresistible picture-book treatments of traditional material that will endlessly enrich our literature for small children." These two books alone would guarantee Leslie Brooke's lasting fame as an illustrator, brimming as they are with vitality and movement and endless amusing and cunning detail. Fortunately, virtually all the artwork has survived, and consequently can now benefit from all the advantages of modern color reproduction, to show more clearly than ever before the sensitivity as well as the boldness of Leslie Brooke's work.

The twinkling comedy of the Johnny Crow books — *Johnny Crow's Garden* (1903), *Johnny Crow's Party* (1907), and *Johnny Crow's New Garden* (1935) — took a final twist when, in a joke silently appreciated by all the Brooke family, the funeral arrangements on Leslie Brooke's death on May 1, 1941 were overseen by the firm of J. Crowe and Sons.

Leslie Brooke's work directly descends from the great illustrators who preceded him, Randolph Caldecott, Walter Crane, and Kate Greenaway, and traces of all three can be seen in his work, as can the influence of Sir John Tenniel, whose drawings Brooke often copied as a child. Among his contemporaries, the most meaningful comparison is probably with Beatrix Potter, whose *The Tale of Peter Rabbit* was published by Warne at Brooke's recommendation. As Joyce Irene Whalley and Tessa Rose Chester put it in their authoritative *History of Children's Book Illustration*, "There were few other picture-book artists in the first twenty years of this century comparable to Beatrix Potter. The only one of her standard who could challenge her in wit and skill and who shared her concern for the integration of word and picture, was L. Leslie Brooke." In the work of Brooke, as of Potter, there is always a direct appeal to the child reader. As for his own influence, it is hard to imagine Maurice Sendak's *Alligators All Around* without *Johnny Crow's Garden*, or Janet and Allan Ahlberg's *Each Peach Pear Plum* without *The Golden Goose Book* and *Ring O' Roses*.

Leslie Brooke's reputation has always been greater in the United States than in his native Britain, largely due to the enthusiastic championship of his work by Anne Carroll Moore, doyenne of children's librarians, and Bertha Mahony Miller, founding editor of the influential journal *The Horn Book*, which devoted its May 1941 issue to an appreciation of Brooke's work. Anne Carroll Moore, Director of Work with Children in the New York Public Library, tirelessly promoted his books, elevating Johnny Crow, as her biographer Frances Clarke Sayers has observed, to "a folk hero among the picture-book set."

Anne Carroll Moore and Leslie Brooke became friends, and she describes their first meeting in a 1921 letter to her niece Rachel: "You would have loved both the home and the studio, everything was so *real*. Mr. Brooke and I literally fell into one another's arms and he wants to give me for myself one of his originals." Leslie Brooke's letters to Anne Carroll Moore record some of his own artistic principles and

influences. In a letter dated September 2, 1941, he quotes W. H. Hunt's advice, "draw firm and be jolly," before going on to discuss the grace and economy of draftsmanship that lie at the root of Randolph Caldecott's, and Leslie Brooke's, greatness: "to see how instinctive the inspiration of the very best type of picture book is, it is worth looking at the very first draft by Caldecott of his *House That Jack Built*. . . . It is just a series of scribbles but implicit in each scrawl can clearly be found the very dog, cat, rat, etc., that has become classic."

Looking at the exquisite new reproductions of Leslie Brooke's subtle watercolors, and admiring once again the clarity and expressiveness of his line drawings, one cannot but agree with Elizabeth Nesbitt's judgment in Virginia Haviland's *Children's Literature: Views and Reviews* that, despite all the marvelous picture books that have appeared in recent years, "the standards of conception and execution set by Randolph Caldecott and Leslie Brooke have not been surpassed."

Neil Philip
PRINCES RISBOROUGH
1992

Index of first lines

Baa, baa Black Sheep   42
Cock-a-doodle doo   13
Gay go up, and gay go down   20
Goosey, Goosey Gander   35
Hickety pickety my black hen   63
Humpty Dumpty sat on a wall   8
Jack and Jill went up the hill   77
Little Bo-Peep has lost her sheep   85
Little Miss Muffet   66
Ring a ring o' roses   6
Simple Simon met a pieman   58
The Lion and the Unicorn   47
The Man in the Moon   25
There was a crooked man,
    and he went a crooked mile   17
There was a little man   74
There was a man, and he had nought   28
This little pig went to market   51
Three wise men of Gotham   70
To market, to market, to buy a fat Pig   39
Wee Willie Winkie runs through the town   89
When good king Arthur ruled this land   81